UNICORNS
OF THE
SECRET STABLE

Heartsong's Missing Foal

JOLLY
FiSH
PRESS

Mendota Heights, Minnesota

By Whitney Sanderson

Illustrated by Jomike Tejido

Book design by Sarah Taplin
Illustrations by Jomike Tejido
Illustrations on pages 8, 61 by North Star Editions

Published in the United States by Jolly Fish Press, an imprint of North Star Editions, Inc.

First Edition
Third Printing, 2020

Library of Congress Cataloging-in-Publication Data (pending)
978-1-63163-392-8 (paperback)
978-1-63163-391-1 (hardcover)

Jolly Fish Press
North Star Editions, Inc.
2297 Waters Drive
Mendota Heights, MN 55120
www.jollyfishpress.com

Printed in the United States of America

TABLE OF CONTENTS

WELCOME TO SUMMERVILLE
Home of Magic Moon Stable . . . **4**

CHAPTER 1
Heartsong . . . **7**

CHAPTER 2
The Fairy Forest . . . **21**

CHAPTER 3
A Wild Ride . . . **43**

CHAPTER 4
Through the Mirror . . . **55**

Welcome to Summerville
Home of Magic Moon Stable

Unicorn Guardians

A long time ago, unicorns and people lived together. When people started hunting the unicorns, two girls decided to help. They used unicorn magic to create a powerful spell. It closed off the Enchanted Realm from the rest of the world. Only the girls' keys could open the Magic Gate.

When the girls grew up, they gave the keys to their daughters. Since then, two young girls have always been the Unicorn Guardians.

CHAPTER 1

Heartsong

I wonder if Heartsong's foal will be a colt or a filly, thought Iris. She hoped it would be a filly, a girl. But a colt would be cute too. He might look like his father, Starfire.

Iris was lost in her daydream. She

didn't hear the *beep, beep, beep* behind her.

Ruby walked into the room. She was

carrying a big bag of powdered sugar.

Streaks of it dusted her face and hair.

"Is that the oven timer?" Ruby asked.

Iris raced to the oven and opened it. The cupcakes on the trays were golden brown. Maybe a little *too* golden brown. But they were not quite burned.

"I was just thinking about Heartsong's foal," Iris said to Ruby. She took the cupcakes out of the oven. "I cannot wait until it is born."

"Me too," said Ruby. "Let's check on the unicorns after we finish making these cupcakes."

The girls' mom walked into the kitchen. She was wearing an apron with pink and green stripes. She smiled. "Are you playing your make-believe game about the unicorns again?" she asked.

Aunt May followed behind her. She wore a matching apron. "Your mom and I used to play that game," she said. "It seems like such a long time ago."

Iris and Ruby reached up to touch the silver keys that hung around their necks. Their mom and Aunt May had once been Unicorn Guardians too. But they had given their keys to the Enchanted Realm to Ruby and Iris. Then, as the Guardians had before them, they had forgotten that unicorns were real.

Now they spent most of their time running their new bakery, the Cupcake Castle. Iris and Ruby liked to help as much as they could.

The girls mixed the frosting and put it into piping bags. They frosted the cupcakes. They topped each one with a fresh blackberry.

Iris carried the cupcakes to the front of the bakery. She put them on a tray behind a sign that read, "Today's Special."

"We are going home now!" Iris called to her mom. "See you later!"

Iris and Ruby hurried through the town of Summerville.

"I wish I had my bike," Ruby said under her breath.

The girls turned down a shady, tree-lined street. Soon, they reached the white farmhouse with the red barn.

They walked up to the pasture gate. The gate was the entrance to the Enchanted Realm. Iris took off the necklace that held her key. She opened the gate.

The girls walked into a meadow filled with wildflowers. A rainbow stretched across the sky. A herd of unicorns grazed nearby.

Iris greeted each unicorn by name. "Hello, Starfire. Hello, Winterlight. Hello, Rainbow Mist." She continued to call each unicorn by name until she reached the last one. She stopped. One unicorn was missing.

Heartsong was gone!

CHAPTER 2

The Fairy Forest

"Unicorns often go into the Fairy Forest to have their foals," Iris read from the *Book of Unicorns*. The book was very old. It had a blue cover with flowers made of real gold. The book had the name of every unicorn in the herd.

It also had advice about caring for unicorns. The book was passed to each new pair of Guardians.

"So we don't need to worry?" asked Ruby.

The girls were in Iris's bedroom, where she kept the book. It really belonged to both of them. But Iris was better at not losing things.

Iris shrugged. "If it's in the book, it must be true," she said. "But Heartsong is the first unicorn to have a foal since we became Guardians."

Unicorns lived for hundreds of years. They only had foals once every twelve years. That was longer than Iris or Ruby had been alive.

"When we go to the Enchanted Realm tomorrow," said Iris, "Heartsong and her new foal will be back."

But she was wrong. Heartsong was still missing the next day.

"The book said that unicorns only spend one night in the Fairy Forest," said Iris. She was worried.

"Look at Starfire," said Ruby. The unicorn stallion was pacing by the edge of the forest.

"Something must be wrong," said Iris. She shivered. The Fairy Forest was full of strange magic. But Iris and Ruby were the Unicorn Guardians. They had to find Heartsong.

Ruby was already walking toward the forest. She was always brave. Iris would have to be brave too—even if she did not feel like it.

It grew dark as they walked into the forest. They could not see the sky through the treetops. The air was growing cold. It felt like they had been walking for hours.

Iris heard a loud neigh from ahead.

She and Ruby ran toward the sound.

Heartsong was in a clearing near a pool of water. Next to her was a tiny, newborn foal. The foal was looking at its reflection in the water.

Heartsong neighed again. She tossed her head. Iris saw that a vine had wrapped around her back leg. Heartsong tried to bite the vine with her teeth, but it was too thick. She was stuck.

Iris walked over to her, talking softly. She tried to untangle the vine. Ruby helped. But as soon as they touched the vine, it began to grow. It became a wild tangle of green. The leaves and stems grew into walls on both sides of them. The walls made a long hall, like in a house.

"Oh no," said Iris. "It's maze weed!"

Iris ran to one end of the green wall. A path led to her left. Another led to the right. The wall was too high to see over or climb.

Ruby pulled Heartsong's leg free from the vine. But the three of them were still stuck in the maze. And Heartsong's foal was outside, all alone!

"Which way do we go?" asked Ruby.

She walked toward Iris. Heartsong followed close behind her.

"I have no idea," said Iris. She felt like crying.

Then she saw a shower of sparks in the sky. They were tiny silver stars. They sparkled and hung in the air.

Ruby pointed. "That's unicorn magic!"

"Heartsong's foal!" said Iris. "It must be making a signal for us."

They walked through the maze, heading toward the stars. They reached a dead end. They had to go back and try another path. But they kept moving in the direction of the shining stars.

At last they found the entrance to the maze. Heartsong's foal was waiting for them near the pool. The cloud of stars shone above its head.

Iris walked over to the foal. It was a filly. Iris touched her soft nose. "Thank you," she said.

The filly nudged her hand. Then she ran to Heartsong on her wobbly, long legs. Heartsong nuzzled her foal.

When she finished, Iris whistled to Heartsong. It was time to go home. The unicorn backed up to the edge of the pool.

Then she whinnied. It was like she did not want to leave.

"Come on, Heartsong," said Iris. "We need to get you and your baby back to the herd."

Heartsong let out a snort that sounded like a sigh. She lowered her head and followed them. Her foal tagged along at her heels.

The girls were quiet as they walked. After a while, Iris said, "I thought of the perfect name for the filly. *Starsong*."

Ruby nodded her head in agreement. "Because she saved us with her stars," she said.

CHAPTER 3

A Wild Ride

The next morning, Iris and Ruby checked on Heartsong and Starsong. Right away, Iris knew something was wrong.

Heartsong galloped along the edge of the Fairy Forest. Little Starsong could barely keep up with her.

Iris was confused. *What could be the matter?* Then she thought of something.

"Ruby," she said. "Who was Heartsong's last foal, before Starsong?"

Ruby frowned. "I think it was Skysong. Or was it Firesong?"

"It was both," said Iris. "Heartsong had twins. What if she had twins this time too?"

Ruby's eyes widened. "If she did, the other foal must still be in the Fairy Forest!"

Iris nodded. "Heartsong does not want to put Starsong in danger by going back," she said.

For a moment, Iris wished she was at the bakery, making cupcakes. She did not want to go back into the forest.

Hooves pounded behind her. Iris turned around. Starfire slid to a stop in front of her. Then he sank down onto one knee and bowed low.

Iris could hardly believe it. Unicorns were wild and proud. They did not usually let people ride them. Starfire must want to help save his foal.

Iris helped Ruby onto Starfire's back. Then she climbed on too. Starfire stood up. Iris held tightly to his mane. Ruby held on to her waist.

Starfire galloped through the forest. He jumped over rocky streams and fallen trees in his path.

Soon, they reached the clearing with the pool. The girls slid down from Starfire's back.

"The foal must be nearby," said Iris. The girls looked behind every tree and rock. But the forest was empty and still.

Starfire lowered his head to drink from the pool. He had no reflection in the water. Ruby walked over and stared into the pool.

"Why can't I see myself?" she asked.

"It must be a mirror lake," said Iris.

"I read about them in the *Book of Unicorns*. Things that fall into the water get trapped in the mirror world. You can only see the reflections of things that have fallen *in*."

Then Iris remembered something. "But I saw a reflection yesterday," she said. "I saw a baby unicorn looking back at the filly. Heartsong's other foal must be trapped in the mirror lake!"

CHAPTER 4

Through the Mirror

Sometimes, Iris did not like being the older sister. It meant that she had to be in charge. She had to come up with a plan.

She walked over to the maze-weed wall.

"Ruby, hold on tight to Starfire's mane," said Iris.

Ruby did what her sister said.

Iris tore a piece off a nearby vine. She put it in Ruby's other hand.

"When I tug twice on this, pull back as hard as you can," she said. "Whatever you do, don't let go."

Iris held the other end of the vine. She took a deep breath. Then she plunged into the water.

She was in a strange world. The pool was not like normal water. She could still breathe. She did not sink. She just sort of drifted. Things drifted past her. Rocks. Leaves. A golden crown. A silver sword. Objects that had been lost in the water.

Iris looked up at the pool's surface. Her own reflection looked back at her.

She could not see Ruby or Starfire. They felt very far away.

Iris searched the pool. There! A baby unicorn was hiding behind a fallen tree in the water.

Iris tried to call to the foal. Silent bubbles rose from her mouth. She reached out her hand and waved to get its attention.

Her motion created tiny waves in the

water. Finally, the foal spotted her.

Slowly, the foal came out from behind the tree. It kicked its legs and swam toward her. Iris grabbed the foal's short mane. She tugged twice on the vine.

She felt herself and the foal being pulled out of the water. The pool seemed to resist. It wanted to keep them. But Starfire was strong. So was Ruby.

Iris's head burst from the water. The foal bobbed beside her. They struggled out onto dry land.

Ruby used her jacket to dry off the foal. This one was a colt. "I have a name for him," she said. "Heart's Mirror."

"It's perfect," said Iris.

When they got back to the meadow, Heartsong galloped over to Heart's Mirror. She nuzzled her foal gently.

Starsong peered shyly at her brother from behind Heartsong. Starfire stood proudly next to his new family.

Later, Iris wrote the foals' names in the *Book of Unicorns*. She wrote about the maze and the mirror lake. Maybe someday their story would help future Guardians.

It was the first time Iris had written in the book. She smiled, thinking about the day's adventures. Now she and Ruby were part of unicorn history too.

THINK ABOUT IT

 Iris and Ruby helped bake cupcakes at the Cupcake Castle. Tell a friend about a time you helped out in the kitchen.

 Iris was afraid to go into the Fairy Forest, but she did it anyway. Write a story about a time you were brave.

 Iris used quick thinking to rescue Heart's Mirror from the mirror lake. What would you have done if you were in the same situation?

ABOUT THE AUTHOR

Whitney Sanderson grew up riding horses as a member of a 4-H club and competing in local jumping and dressage shows. She has written several books in the Horse Diaries chapter book series. She is also the author of *Horse Rescue: Treasure*, based on her time volunteering at an equine rescue farm. She lives in Massachusetts.

ABOUT THE ILLUSTRATOR

Jomike Tejido is an author and illustrator of the picture book *There Was an Old Woman Who Lived in a Book*. He also illustrated the Pet Charms and My Magical Friends leveled reader series. He has fond memories of horseback riding as a kid and has always loved drawing magical creatures. Jomike lives in Manila with his wife, two daughters, and a chow chow named Oso.

RETURN TO MAGIC MOON STABLE

Book 1

Book 2

Book 3

Book 4

AVAILABLE NOW